Frog Goes

written by Stan Cullimore

illustrated by Louise Gardner

In the park, there is a pond.

Pond

Play park

Park keeper

Dog

In the pond, there is a frog.

Hole

Frog

Ducks

His name is Fred.

He never leaves the pond.

This is why ...

It all started when Fred decided to go on holiday.

5

13

19

So Fred went back to the pond.

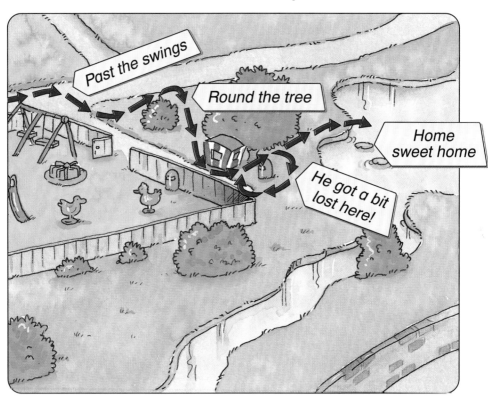

You know what?

He never **did** leave the pond ever again.